D1515338

First published in Persian © 2010 Nazar Publisher, Tehran, Iran.
This edition first published in the United States in 2019
by Tiny Owl Publishing, London, U.K.

www.tinyowl.co.uk

Translated by Azita Rassi
© 2015 Tiny Owl Publishing Ltd

A CIP record for this book is available from the Library of Congress.

ISBN 978-1-910328-49-1

Printed in China

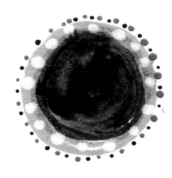

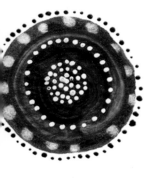

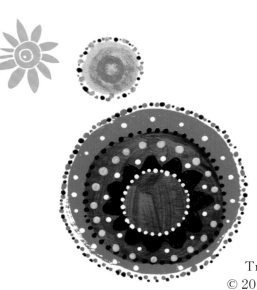
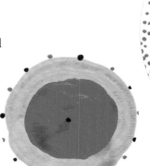

when I
Colored in
the World

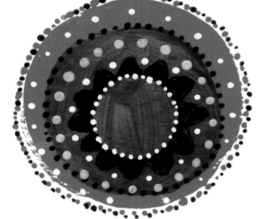

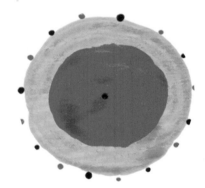

Ahmadreza Ahmadi

Illustrated by Ehsan Abdollahi

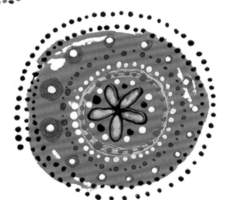

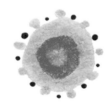

TINY OWL

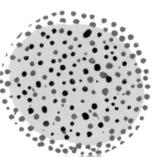

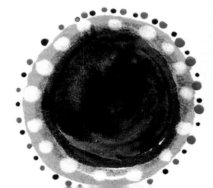

My mom gave me a box of crayons for coloring,
and an eraser to rub things out with. So guess what I did?

Desert

I rubbed out the word **desert**.
I wrote the word **roses**.

Roses

Red

With my red crayon I made roses grow all over the world!

I gave the world red.

Darkness

I rubbed out the word **darkness**.
I wrote the word light with my yellow crayon.

Light
Yellow

With my yellow crayon I made lights
come on all over the world!

I gave the world yellow.

Boredom

I rubbed out the word **boredom**.
I got my blue crayon and I wrote playing.

Playing
Sky blue

All over the world people played.

I gave the world sky blue.

Drought

I rubbed out the word drought.
I wrote rain with my silver crayon.

Silver
Rain

I made it rain all over the world, and
everyone had to put up umbrellas!

I gave the world silver.

Hunger

I rubbed out the word hunger.
I wrote wheat with my green crayon.

Green
Wheat

I made wheat grow in fields all over
the world.

I gave the world green.

war

I rubbed out the word war.
I got my light blue crayon and I wrote peace with it.

Light blue
Peace

All over the world news came from
radios saying that all the wars had stopped.
After that news, the radios played such lovely
music that flowers bloomed in empty vases.

I gave the world light blue.

winter

I rubbed out the word winter.
I used my orange crayon to write spring.

Orange
Spring

All over the world, snow melted.
Primroses and violets and orange blossoms
flowered so that children could sleep with
a lovely flowery scent all around them.

I gave the world orange.

Noise

I rubbed out the word noise.
I wrote song with my dark blue crayon.

Dark blue
Song

All over the world my song made children
so happy that they danced.

I gave the world dark blue.

Crying

I rubbed out the word crying.
Instead I wrote laughter with my purple crayon.

Purple
Laughter

Now, all over the world, mothers danced
and laughed with their children.

I gave the world purple.

Storm

I rubbed out the word storm.
In its place I wrote breeze with my violet crayon.

Violet
Breeze

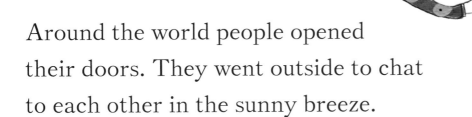

Around the world people opened
their doors. They went outside to chat
to each other in the sunny breeze.

I gave the world violet.

Illness

I rubbed out the word illness.
I got my pink crayon, and I wrote health instead.

Pink

Health

All over the world people who had been ill were
suddenly well! They ran with their friends and
were happy.

I gave the world pink.

old age

I rubbed out the words old and age.
Instead I used my orange crayon to write people.

Orange
People

And all over the world, nobody minded at all
whether somebody else was old or young.
They were just interested in each other.

I gave the world orange.

Flood

I rubbed out the word flood.
Instead I wrote drizzle with my silver crayon,
just as I had used it to write rain.

Silver

Drizzle

Around the world, harvests were saved.

I gave the world silver.

Despair

I rubbed out the word despair.
I wrote hope with my yellow crayon.

Yellow

Hope

All over the world children smiled.
They ran into the fields and up the hills
looking at the beautiful new life growing all around.

I gave the world hope.

Can you change the world?

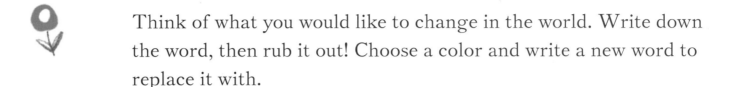

Think of what you would like to change in the world. Write down the word, then rub it out! Choose a color and write a new word to replace it with.

Colors can make you feel different emotions like happy, sad, or angry. What color is the new word? How does it make you feel? What colors don't you like?

Write your own poem with all the new words you have chosen to make the world a better place. Pick your favorite colors and draw the things that make you happy.

For more ideas and worksheets visit www.tinyowl.co.uk

About the author

Ahmadreza Ahmadi is one of Iran's greatest contemporary poets. He has written numerous children's books, some of which have won major literary awards in Iran. In 2010, he was among the five shortlisted nominees for the Hans Christian Andersen award.